E   Peet, Bill.
PEE   Cock-a-doodle
         Dudley

DATE DUE			

COCK-A-DOODLE
DUDLEY

COCK-A-DOODLE DUDLEY

BILL PEET

Houghton Mifflin Company Boston

Library of Congress Cataloging-in-Publication Data

Peet, Bill.
    Cock-a-doodle Dudley/Bill Peet.
        p.   cm.
    Summary: Dudley the rooster's ability to make the sun rise with
his crowing is questioned by a spiteful goose, whose malice almost
destroys the popular rooster.
    HC ISBN 0-395-55331-8   PA ISBN 0-395-65745-8
    [1. Roosters—Fiction. 2. Domestic animals—Fiction.] I. Title.
PZ7.P353Cm   1990   90-32739
[E]—dc20   CIP
                            AC

Printed in the United States of America
WOZ   10 9 8 7 6 5 4

With fond memories of Dear Aunt Ella,
a special friend during my boyhood

Dudley was always up before dawn, perched on a fencepost and ready to crow at the first glimpse of the sun.

For such a scraggly-tailed runt of a rooster, he was a surprisingly powerful crower. He could crow louder and longer than any rooster for miles around.

His crowing was much more than a cock-a-doodle-do. Dudley carried on with beautiful trills and tremolos that echoed far across the countryside.

Such a spirited, enthusiastic greeting delighted old Sol,
the sun, and he always rose above the horizon beaming with
pleasure, wearing a big broad smile for Dudley, who was by far his
favorite rooster.

Dudley was also a great favorite with everyone in the barnyard. His neighbors believed his spectacular crowing was magic, with miraculous power to make the sun rise.

When he took his morning stroll, Dudley was showered with praise and gratitude for creating a new day.

"You've done it again, Dudley," said Trevor the turkey. "Nice crowin'."

"You're a wonder," said Ludwig the pig.

"A remarkable rooster," said Hector the plowhorse.

"He's marvelous! Dudley's fabulous!" chorused all the hens. "Dudley is adorable!"

The rooster was a favorite with everyone but Gunther, a bad-tempered old goose.

Gunther was fiercely jealous and was
always itching for a fight. "Adorable Dudley!" he scoffed.
"Cock-a-doodle Dudley! Dudley the great! How about you and me
having a showdown to see who's the greatest, you skinny little
nothing of a rooster!"

Dudley didn't dare match words with the brute of a goose.
He always pretended not to hear, but went on his way out to the
vegetable garden and slipped through the picket fence, where
potbellied Gunther could not follow.

Out there he could be alone and enjoy a breakfast of snails and caterpillars and talk to himself.

"I feel silly when I get all that praise for something I could never do," he said. "How could they ever get the outlandish idea that my crowing is magic and makes the sun rise? Anyway, I'm going to set them straight. Maybe I'll tell them tomorrow."

"Why wait till tomorrow?" someone said.

Dudley looked frantically around until he spied the big goose with his neck stretched through the picket fence. The old bird had heard every word!

"I'm going to tell them today! Right away!" Gunther
said, and he went waddling off to the barnyard.

"I'm a ruined rooster!" exclaimed Dudley. "That goose
will fix me good! I'll be an outcast. No one will ever speak
to me again. But if I'm going to be ruined, I might as
well have my say."

When Dudley reached the barnyard, Gunther was perched on a stack of hay bales, shouting to get attention. "Hear this! Hear this, everyone!" As soon as he had attracted a crowd he lowered his voice. "Friends," he said, "there is something you must know. We have a phony rooster in our midst. A faker! A fraud!"

"Oh no! Not Dudley!" cried Trevor. "No, no!"

"Yes, I mean Dudley," said the goose. "His crowing has no more magic than a pig's oink. He has nothing to do with the sun's coming up. I heard him say so."

"Why should we believe you?" said Hector the horse. "You've always been jealous of Dudley."

Then they all cut loose on the goose, with everyone shouting at once. "*You* are the phony one! You're an old windbag! A grouch and a grump! A pompous old nincompoop! A mean old Scrooge!"

"Hold it! Hold it!" cried Dudley. "Please! Please, listen! Let me have my say!"

Quickly Dudley hopped up beside Gunther to face his friends. "The goose is right," he said. "I'm sorry to tell you that I have no special magic. My crowing doesn't make the sun rise. Crowing is my way of greeting my old friend Sol, the sun — just my way of celebrating a new day, that's all. I'm just a plain, ordinary rooster."

For a minute everyone stared at Dudley in silence, too befuddled for words.

Finally Hector spoke up. "No need to be sorry, my friend. None of us can do anything special. We are ordinary too. I'm nothing but a plain, ordinary plowhorse."

"I'm just an ordinary old porker," said Ludwig the pig.

"I've got fancy tailfeathers," said Trevor the turkey. "Otherwise I'm just a plain old turkey."

"We're all ordinary!" chorused the hens. "Hooray for ordinary Dudley! He is terrifically ordinary! Hooray! Hooray! Dudley's okay!"

Dudley was just as popular as ever, and old Gunther the goose was furious. "I still say Dudley's a phony," he muttered, "and I'll peck him to a frazzle the first chance I get."

The angry goose saw his chance one afternoon when he spied Dudley out in the meadow chasing dragonflies. When he was sure no one was watching, Gunther slipped through the fence, then in a low crouch he went scooting through the tall weeds, straight for the rooster.

If Dudley hadn't caught sight of him at the last
second, Gunther would have snatched him by the tailfeathers.
The rooster could easily have outrun the big goose if it hadn't

been for the tall, wiry weeds, which kept tripping him up.
Gunther kept coming full speed, gaining with every step, and
just as he was about to catch Dudley . . .

. . . they suddenly came to a dark, spooky woods. Gunther wasn't nearly brave enough to go into the spooky place, but Dudley kept on running. He knew he would be in danger in the woods, but he would rather take a chance than be pecked to a frazzle by the brute of a goose.

And Dudley *was* in danger! The instant he entered the woods he nearly ran head on into a fox.

Just as the fox pounced, the rooster fluttered straight up
in the air, just high enough to land on a tree limb.

He was beyond the reach of the fox, but he wasn't safe from the owls who would be out hunting in the woods after dark.

It was getting near sundown. Before old Sol slipped below the horizon, he made a big decision. "If my favorite rooster doesn't crow in the morning, I'm not comin' up! There'll be no day tomorrow."

Sure enough, as soon as it grew dark, great horned owls swooped silently through the trees, searching for anything that moved. For once Dudley was grateful to be a skinny little nothing of a rooster.

He scrunched himself flat against the tree trunk, wide-eyed
with fright, hoping to last through the night without being
seen. It was a long night, since Dudley didn't dare to do
any crowing or make even the slightest sound.

When the sun didn't show up at his usual time the next morning, the farm animals guessed something must be wrong. But they couldn't be sure until the farmer came out into his back yard and stared at the eastern sky.

"Doggone," he muttered. "Nearly nine o'clock, and the sun's not up! Something's gone haywire. Not even a rooster crow!"

"Strange indeed," said Hector. "No rooster crow! Where's Dudley? Has anyone seen him? Gunther, didn't I hear you threaten to peck Dudley to a frazzle?"

"W-w-well, y-y-yes," stammered the goose. "B-b-but I didn't. All I did was chase him a little way."

"Chase him to where?" snorted Hector. "Tell me before I kick the stuffing out of you!"

"He ran into Warwick's woods," said Gunther, "yesterday afternoon."

Hector nudged open the barnyard gate, and as he went galloping off over the meadow he shouted, "If I don't come back with the rooster, you'd better be gone, Gunther!"

When he approached the dense woods, the horse realized that he had no chance of finding Dudley unless Dudley was alive and could answer when Hector called his name.

"Dudley! Dudley!" called the horse as he went stumbling through the darkness, bumbling into trees and tripping over logs and stumps. He kept circling aimlessly around in the woods, calling and calling: "Dudley! Dudley! Dudley!" But the only replies were the echoes of his own voice.

Dudley didn't dare answer him. A huge owl was
perched on a tree limb just above the rooster, and he couldn't do
much more than breathe. His only hope was for Hector to come
close enough to his tree so he could leap onto the horse's
back. It was all a matter of luck.

Luck was with Dudley on that long, long night. Hector finally came stumbling through the darkness directly under his tree limb, and the rooster leaped onto his back, shouting, "Hector! It's me, Dudley! Turn on the speed!"

If the owl hadn't been so stupefied at the sight of a rooster riding horseback, he could have swooped down and snatched Dudley in a flash.

As they crossed the meadow, Hector asked Dudley, "Do you notice anything strange about today?"

"Today!" exclaimed Dudley. "You mean tonight, don't you?"

"No, no!" said Hector. "It is after nine in the morning and the sun's not up! I'm taking you back to your favorite fence-post so you can crow the sun up."

"But you know my crowing is worthless," said Dudley. "No more magic than the pig's oink."

"This is no time to quibble," said Hector.

When they reached the barnyard, the turkey, the pig, and all the chickens were overjoyed to see Dudley back all in one piece. They burst into happy cheering: "Dudley! Dudley! Hooray for Cock-a-doodle Dudley! Dudley the great! Hooray! Hooray!"

Finally Hector interrupted them. "Hold it! I hate to be a killjoy, but I believe Dudley is eager to do some crowing."

"Very well," said Dudley, "but don't expect too much." Then he took a deep, deep breath, stood on tiptoes, and let go with a mighty crow.

Dudley's magical crowing worked instantly. Up bounced the sun, all the way to where he should be at nine-fifteen and with an enormous smile on his face just for his favorite rooster. Of course, the spectacular sunrise called for more cheering and more praise for the magical Dudley.

As for Gunther the goose, he had been afraid that Hector would come back without the rooster, so he had left in a hurry.